Happy Holidays!
Love,
Mrs. Kellough

The Missing Pony Pal

Do you love ponies? Be a Pony Pal!

Look for these Pony Pal books:

PONY PALS

The Missing Pony Pal

Jeanne Betancourt

illustrated by Paul Bachem

A
LITTLE APPLE
PAPERBACK

SCHOLASTIC INC.
New York Toronto London Auckland Sydney

ISBN 0-590-37459-1

12 11 10 9 8 7 6 5   9/9 0 1 2/0

Printed in the U.S.A.   40

First Scholastic printing, September 1997

Thank you to Barbara Byron, Gerrie and Brie Giunta, Cindy and Heather Murphy, Jendia Marlowe and Morgan, Hannan Al Tagir and Cricket. They all helped me with the research for this Pony Pal story.

Contents

The Missing Pony Pal

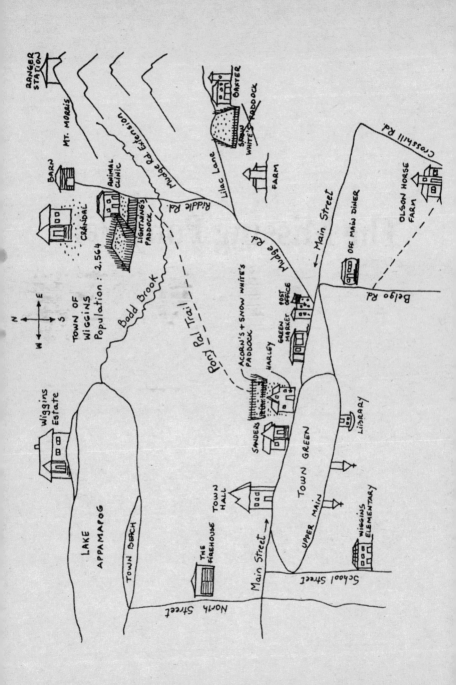

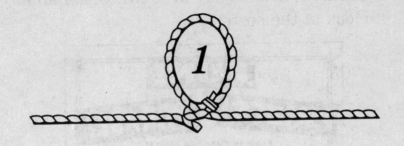

Egg and Spoon

Lulu Sanders ran all the way to the grocery store. She and her Pony Pal, Anna Harley, needed carrots and apples for their ponies. Anna taught her pony, Acorn, tricks with carrot rewards. Lulu's pony, Snow White, liked carrots, too. But apples were Snow White's favorite treat.

Lulu was paying for the apples and carrots when she saw Mr. Olson. He owned a horse farm and was a friend of the Pony Pals. Mr. Olson was pinning up a poster.

Lulu went over to say hi to Mr. Olson and to look at the poster.

FUN!
PRIZES! PARADE!

COME TO THE PONY GAMES!

GYMKHANA AND
COSTUME PARADE
SEPTEMBER 20th 9:00 A.M.
AT OLSON HORSE FARM
CROSSHILL ROAD, WIGGINS

GAMES
★Bending Race   ★Carton Race
★Egg and Spoon   ★Ring on Cone Race
★Hurtle Race   ★Litter Race
★Stepping Stone Dash ★Sack Race
★Old Sock Race

COSTUME PARADE
PRIZES FOR COSTUMES

"A gymkhana!" exclaimed Lulu. "Those games are so much fun."

Mr. Olson handed Lulu a poster. "Here's one for the Pony Pals," he said. "I hope you'll all come."

"We will," said Lulu.

Lulu thanked Mr. Olson and left the store with the grocery bag and poster. She couldn't wait to tell Anna about the pony games.

Anna was in the paddock grooming Acorn. Snow White was grazing nearby.

"Anna, I have the best news!" shouted Lulu.

Lulu showed Anna the poster and told her about the games. Snow White ran up to Lulu and sniffed at the grocery bag. She laughed. "You're right," she told her pony. "I've got some apples for you." Lulu gave Snow White an apple and Acorn a carrot.

Anna and Lulu talked about the gymkhana while they saddled up their ponies. Lulu was still talking about the games as they rode onto Pony Pal Trail. The trail started behind Anna's house and went for a mile and a half through the woods. It ended at a field behind Pam Crandal's house.

Lulu and Snow White came out of the

woods into the Crandals' big sunny field. Lulu saw five poles standing in a row down the middle of the field. Pam was riding Lightning in and out of the poles.

Anna rode up beside Lulu. "What's Pam doing?" Anna asked.

"She practicing the Bending Race," Lulu told Anna. "She must already know about the gymkhana."

When Pam saw Anna and Lulu she galloped Lightning in a straight line toward them. "I have the best news!" yelled Pam.

"We know," said Lulu. She reached into her saddlebag, pulled out the poster, and held it up for Pam to see.

"That was my news!" said Pam. "Isn't it great? Our ponies are going to do so well."

The girls moved their ponies into a tight circle and studied the poster.

"Playing those games sounds like so much fun," said Anna. "But I only know a couple of them."

"I know most of them," said Lulu. "When I lived in England we had gymkhanas all

the time. I'm not sure about some of the rules though."

"My mother said she'd help us," said Pam. "She teaches the games to her riding students. She even lent me her stopwatch so we can time ourselves."

"You win by how fast you play the games," Lulu told Anna.

"And for some games you work in relay teams," Pam said.

"We'll be a team," said Anna. "The Pony Pal Team."

"The Sack Race is my favorite," said Lulu.

"How do you play the Sack Race?" asked Anna.

"You ride with an empty grain sack in one hand and your reins in the other," Lulu explained. "You halt your pony at the center of the field, jump off your pony, and put your feet and legs into the bag. You have to hold the bag up with one hand and your pony's bridle with the other. Then you hop to the finish line with your pony walking beside you. It's really hard, but fun."

"Acorn might think the bag has grain and try to eat it!" said Anna.

"That always happens in the Sack Race," giggled Lulu.

"Let's practice the Bending Race first," said Pam. "My mom helped me draw the course to show us where to go."

The Pony Pals rode to the starting line. They dismounted and studied Pam's drawing of the course.

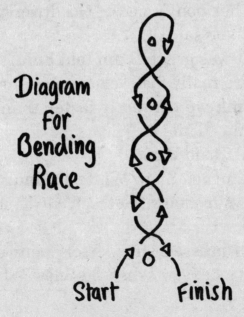

Diagram
For
Bending
Race

Start   Finish

"Let's walk our ponies through the course before we ride," suggested Lulu. "I don't want Snow White to be frightened by the poles."

The girls led their ponies in and out of the row of poles. Then they mounted and took turns riding the same course. Lulu and Snow White went last.

Lulu loved how it felt to go fast and lean around the poles. When she reached the finish line she brought Snow White to a walk. They were both breathing hard. She patted her pony's neck. "Good work, Snow White," she said.

"That was great," Pam told Lulu.

"You're really fast!" exclaimed Anna.

"I think we can do it faster than that," said Lulu. "Time us."

"Okay," said Pam.

Lulu turned Snow White around.

"On your mark. Get set. GO!" shouted Pam.

Lulu pressed her heels into Snow White's side. "Go!" she told Snow White.

Snow White galloped toward the first pole and bent around it.

"Faster!" Lulu told her pony. "Faster!"

Snow White bent around the second pole.

"Come on, Snow White," said Lulu. Lulu pulled on the reins to tell Snow White to bend closer to the pole.

Suddenly, Snow White slipped and fell. Lulu was thrown from the saddle and went flying through the air. Lulu hit the ground with a thud. Everything went black.

X Rays

When Lulu opened her eyes, Mrs. Crandal was looking down at her. "What happened?" Lulu asked.

Mrs. Crandal put her hand on Lulu's arm. "Don't move, Lulu," she said. "You had a bad fall."

Lulu rested her head back on the ground. She looked around. "Where's Snow White?" she asked. "Where's my pony?"

"She fell, too," said Mrs. Crandal. "Pam is taking her to the barn. Anna went to look for Dr. Crandal. He'll take good care of

Snow White." Mrs. Crandal smiled. "See how handy it is to have a veterinarian in the family?"

Lulu nodded, but she didn't smile back. She was too worried about Snow White. She tried to get up again. "I want to see Snow White now," she said.

"Please, don't move, Lulu," said Mrs. Crandal. "Tell me what hurts."

Lulu lay back. "My leg hurts," she said.

"An ambulance is coming," Mrs. Crandal said. "You blacked out and we don't know what's happened to your leg. We need to have you checked out."

Lulu swallowed back tears. "I don't want to go to the hospital," she said. "I want to see Snow White."

Mrs. Crandal held Lulu's hand. "I know," she said. "But you can't right now. Please, try not to worry, honey."

Anna came up to Lulu and squatted beside her. "You okay?" she asked.

"I'm okay," said Lulu. "How's Snow White?"

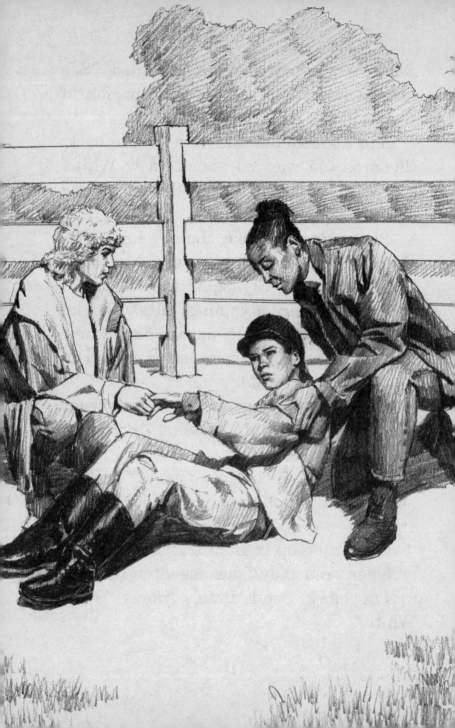

"We don't know yet," said Anna. "Dr. Crandal was on a barn call. We beeped him and he's on his way."

"Here comes the ambulance," Mrs. Crandal said.

"Can I go in the ambulance with her?" asked Anna.

"Good idea," said Mrs. Crandal. "I'll follow with my car. But first I'm going to call Lulu's grandmother."

A man and woman came over to Lulu. They put a big white soft collar around her neck. Then they slid a board underneath her. "We need to keep you still until you're checked for injuries at the hospital," the woman told her. "It's the safest way to deal with a fall like yours."

"My pony is hurt, too," Lulu told them.

"We've never taken a pony in the ambulance," said the man with a smile. "It would take a mighty big collar."

"I'm sure Doctor Crandal will take good care of your pony," said the woman.

"He's a terrific vet," said the man.

"I know," said Lulu. She tried to smile.

The man and woman picked up the stretcher and carried Lulu to the ambulance. Anna climbed in and sat near Lulu.

The ambulance pulled out of the Crandals' driveway. Lulu knew that the red light on top was flashing. She'd seen the town ambulance taking other people to the hospital. But now *she* was the one inside the fast-moving van.

Lulu felt tired, her leg hurt, and she was scared. She closed her eyes. She wondered if her leg was broken. What if Snow White's leg is broken? she thought. That would be even worse.

Lulu opened her eyes. Anna was looking at her. Lulu could see that her friend was worried, too. "Pam is staying with Snow White," Anna told her. Lulu nodded and closed her eyes again.

Lulu knew how lucky she was to have good friends like Anna and Pam. She had only been living in Wiggins a short time, but it felt like the Pony Pals had been together forever.

Lulu's father grew up in Wiggins. Her grandmother said even when he was little he liked to study animals. Now he was a naturalist, studying and writing about wild animals. Lulu's mother was a naturalist, too, but she died when Lulu was four years old. After her mother died, Lulu traveled everywhere with her father. Lulu loved traveling and learning about different animals. When she turned ten, her father said it was time for her to live in one place, and Lulu moved in with her grandmother. Lulu thought living in Wiggins would be boring — until she met Anna and Pam and became a Pony Pal.

Pam and Anna had been best friends since kindergarten but they were very different. Pam was tall and Anna was short. Pam got the best marks in school and was always very organized. Anna was dyslexic, so reading and writing were difficult for her. Anna was a terrific artist and Pam couldn't draw anything! Lulu loved Anna's drawings and paintings, especially the ones she did of ponies and horses. Though they each liked different things, all the Pony Pals loved ponies and riding.

The ambulance came to a stop. Lulu opened her eyes. "We're at the hospital," said Anna.

For the next half hour Lulu was too busy to think about her Pony Pals or worry about Snow White. A doctor and a nurse were asking her questions like, "What's your name?" and "What month is it?" Lulu knew they were making sure she hadn't hurt her brain in the fall.

The nurse took her blood pressure and pulse. She was really nice and told Lulu that she had had a pony once. The doctor checked Lulu's body from head to toe. "She's looking for broken bones or internal injuries," the nurse told Lulu.

"I don't feel any injuries," said Dr. Rice.

"Now, Lulu, we're going to take the collar off and pull out that board. But I'd like you to stay on the stretcher. We're going to X-ray your leg."

During the X ray Lulu started to worry about Snow White again. A broken leg for a pony was more serious than a broken leg for a person. A pony with a broken leg might die. I'd rather have my leg broken than Snow White's, thought Lulu.

An X-ray technician wheeled Lulu out of the X-ray room into the hallway. Anna, Mrs. Crandal, and Lulu's grandmother were waiting there for her.

Grandmother Sanders bent over and kissed Lulu on the forehead. "You poor dear," she said. "I always said that horseback riding is too dangerous for young girls."

Lulu loved her grandmother, but they had different ideas about what girls should do.

Dr. Rice came over to them. "How would

17

you like to get off that stretcher now?" she asked Lulu.

"Can I?" Lulu asked.

Dr. Rice nodded. "No broken bones. But you do have a bad bruise on your thigh."

The nurse helped Lulu off the stretcher. She was glad to be standing up again, but her leg still hurt.

"That bruise will turn red and purple," said Dr. Rice. "You should ice it twenty minutes every two hours until you go to bed tonight." Dr. Rice gave Lulu a special bandage to hold the ice. "In a couple of weeks you'll be good as new."

"Thank goodness," said Grandmother Sanders.

"When can she ride again?" asked Anna.

"As soon as she wants," answered the doctor. "But she's going to feel sore on that leg."

"I don't think she should ever ride again," said Grandmother Sanders.

"Lulu's a Pony Pal," said Anna.

"And an excellent rider," added Mrs. Crandal. "Accidents happen."

Lulu didn't care about what they were saying about riding. She just wanted to know how Snow White was. "I want to go back to your place now," she told Mrs. Crandal. "I want to see Snow White."

A Magical Horse

Mrs. Crandal parked the car near the Crandals' long barn. Lulu hesitated for a moment. What if Snow White were seriously hurt? A tear started to form in the corner of her eye. Lulu got out of the car. She couldn't wait to see her pony. Lulu felt her heart pounding with fear as she walked down the barn aisle. Snow White wasn't in any of the stalls. Maybe her pony was having an operation. Maybe she was . . .

Anna pointed. "There's Snow White," she said. "She's in the last stall."

"Snow White, I'm here," Lulu called.

Snow White answered Lulu with a weak whinny. Lulu's leg hurt, but she still tried to run to her pony.

Dr. Crandal and Pam were in the stall with Snow White. There was a big bandage on her left front leg.

Dr. Crandal smiled at Lulu. "Looks like you're doing okay, Lulu," he said.

"I am," said Lulu. "How's Snow White?"

"I think she'll be okay, too," said Dr. Crandal. "She sprained the tendon in her foreleg, but it's not broken."

"Thank goodness," said Mrs. Crandal.

Pam patted Snow White's side. "She's such a good pony," said Pam.

Lulu threw her arms around Snow White. "I was so worried about you," she said. Snow White nuzzled Lulu's hair. Tears filled Lulu's eyes. "Thank you, Dr. Crandal. Thank you for taking care of her."

"No trouble," he said. "But you two must have taken quite a tumble. What happened?"

"I was making Snow White go too fast," said Lulu. "And I leaned over too far."

"Well, you're lucky," he said. "Snow White could have easily broken her leg."

"I know," said Lulu softly. "It was all my fault."

"It could have happened to anyone," said Pam.

"We all fall once in awhile," said Mrs. Crandal.

"I shouldn't have made her go so fast," said Lulu.

Anna put her hand on Lulu's shoulder. "It wasn't your fault."

"Snow White should rest for a few days," advised Dr. Crandal. "And I'd like her to spend the night here. I want you to take off her bandage every four hours during the day and hose the injured area with cold water. During the night, you can let her rest."

"I'll do anything to make Snow White better," Lulu said.

Pam jumped up on the stall gate. "Can we have a barn sleepover tonight?" she asked. "That way we can all help take care of Snow White."

"Of course," said Mrs. Crandal.

"Can Snow White still be in the gymkhana?" Anna asked.

"It's in two weeks," added Pam.

"I think she'll be healed by then," said Dr. Crandal.

"Great!" said Anna. "Tonight, let's work on ideas for our costumes."

The Pony Pals had dinner with Pam's family. Lulu tried to eat her spaghetti and have a good time like everyone else. But every time she remembered the accident her stomach turned over.

After dinner the girls went to the barn to take care of Snow White. They unwrapped her bandage and Lulu hosed down the injured leg with cold water. She could see

Snow White's foreleg was very swollen. Lulu carefully put the bandage back on.

"Let's go to the office and make a list of costume ideas for the gymkhana games," said Anna.

"And what we need to make them," said Pam.

"I'll draw pictures," added Anna.

But Lulu didn't feel like talking about costumes. "I'm going to stay with Snow White for a little while," she told her friends. "You can go work on the costume ideas. I'll be there in a minute."

Lulu stood alone at the stall door and watched Snow White for a long while. Snow White fell asleep. Suddenly, the injured pony shivered and moaned. She's having a nightmare about the accident, thought Lulu. Lulu went back into the stall and stroked her pony's cheek. "Snow White," she whispered. "It's all right. You're having a bad dream."

Snow White opened her eyes. Lulu could

see the fear in her brown eyes. "It's just a dream," said Lulu. "You're okay." Snow White's body relaxed and she closed her eyes again. Lulu put her head against Snow White's side. She could feel her pony's heartbeat. "Good night, Snow White," she said softly. "I'm sorry."

Pam and Anna were laughing when Lulu came into the office.

"Lulu, look at this," said Anna. She held up a drawing.

"And this one," said Pam. She held up another drawing for Lulu to see.

Lulu managed to laugh with her friends over the funny drawings. But she didn't feel happy. She was thinking, I made Snow White go too fast. It's my fault she is hurt.

"We came up with a neat idea for you and Snow White," said Anna.

"It was Anna's idea and it is *so* great," added Pam.

"We think Snow White would make a *perfect* unicorn," said Anna. "And you could be a princess."

"Do you like it?" said Pam. "Snow White really looks like a magical horse."

"It's okay," said Lulu. She knew she didn't sound very excited. But she couldn't help it. She didn't feel like being in a costume parade. "What about you?" Lulu asked. "What are you going to be?"

Pam and Anna told Lulu all their ideas for costumes and how they would make them. They had tons of ideas but couldn't decide which ones were best. Lulu was hardly listening. She couldn't pay attention.

Before long, Pam turned out the lights and the girls slipped into their sleeping bags. Pam and Anna talked some more about the gymkhana and how much fun it was going to be. Finally, they fell asleep. But Lulu couldn't fall asleep. She was thinking about the accident. I almost broke Snow White's leg, she thought. What if I hurt my pony again?

Afraid!

After breakfast the next morning Dr. Crandal checked on Snow White. The Pony Pals watched as he unwrapped the pony's bandage, squeezed the injured area, and picked up her hoof. Snow White gently nuzzled the top of the doctor's shoulder. He patted her on the head.

"Snow White's leg is healing nicely, Lulu," Dr. Crandal said. "But leave the bandage on for another day. You can take her home whenever you want."

"Thank you, Dr. Crandal," said Lulu. She

was happy that Snow White would be all right.

"When can Lulu ride Snow White again?" asked Pam.

"I'll check her on Tuesday," said Dr. Crandal. "You can probably be on her after that. But take it easy the first few days."

"Can Snow White practice for the gymkhana?" asked Anna.

"She should be able to by Saturday," Dr. Crandal answered, as he packed up his medical bag. Before he left, Dr. Crandal smiled at Lulu. "But don't try to break any more records, young lady."

"I won't," promised Lulu.

"Let's practice games today," said Anna.

"My mother said you could ride Paint until Snow White's better," Pam told Lulu. "And no one's taking lessons on him today."

"Paint will love the games," Anna said.

"I don't feel like riding today," said Lulu.

"It's important to ride as soon as possible after you fall off a horse," said Pam.

"I know," said Lulu. "But not today."

"Snow White won't mind if you ride another pony," said Anna.

"You've ridden the school ponies a lot," added Pam. "You even helped train Paint."

Lulu leaned against Snow White's side. "I told you I don't want to ride today," she said.

"Does your leg still hurt?" asked Anna.

"A little," answered Lulu. "I don't think I should ride."

Pam walked over to Lulu. "You can be our coach then," she said.

"Okay," Lulu agreed.

Lulu helped Anna and Pam saddle up Lightning and Acorn and they all went to the big field.

"Walk the Bending Race again before you gallop," Lulu told her friends.

"We don't need to walk it again," said Pam. "We did Bending Race a lot yesterday."

"If I'm the coach you have to do what I say," said Lulu. She took her whistle from her pocket and hung it around her neck.

"And if I blow the whistle you should halt immediately. It's for safety."

Pam rolled her eyes. "Okay, coach," said Pam.

"Aye, aye, sir," giggled Anna.

Pam and Anna took turns doing Bending Poles at a walk.

"Now can we do it for real?" Anna asked Lulu.

"I guess," said Lulu.

Pam pulled Lightning up to the starting line. "Use the timer," she told Lulu.

"We're going to do it without the timer first," said Lulu. "Are you ready?"

Pam nodded.

"On your mark," said Lulu. "Get set. Go!"

Pam and Lightning were off. They bent around the poles at a gallop. Lulu watched them nervously. As they sped around the poles on the return trip, Lulu blew the whistle. Pam slowed Lightning and halted.

"What's wrong?" shouted Pam.

"You're leaning too far," yelled Lulu.

Pam walked Lightning back to the start-

33

ing line. "It didn't feel like we were leaning too far," said Pam.

"It didn't look like it to me, either," said Anna.

"Well, it wasn't safe riding," said Lulu. "You should be more careful."

Next, Acorn and Anna galloped through the course.

Lulu blew the whistle again. Anna halted Acorn. "Don't go so fast!" yelled Lulu.

"It is a *race*," Pam told Lulu. "You're supposed to go fast."

"They were going *too* fast," said Lulu. "They could get hurt."

Anna pulled Acorn up next to Lulu. "Acorn likes to go fast," she told Lulu. "And we've galloped in and out of poles before."

Lulu scowled at Anna. "It's safer to go slow," she said.

Pam dismounted. "Let's practice a different game," she said.

"You can teach us that Sack Race," said Anna.

"Good idea," said Lulu. "First, practice hopping in the sack while the ponies have a rest."

"They're not tired," mumbled Anna. "We've only been riding fifteen minutes."

"They can rest while we go find sacks," sighed Pam. She handed Lightning's reins over to Lulu.

Lulu stayed with the two ponies while Anna and Pam went to find empty grain sacks. She looked out at the field and thought about her accident. She remembered the feeling of going fast. And the awful feeling of falling. But mostly, she remembered how scared she felt.

Lulu heard laughter behind her. She turned around. Pam and Anna were hopping toward her in grain sacks.

Acorn whinnied excitedly. When Anna reached him, he nuzzled the sack. "That tickles," laughed Anna. Anna took Acorn's reins from Lulu and hopped with Acorn beside her. Acorn tried to poke his nose in the sack again. This time he knocked Anna

35

over. Anna rolled on the ground laughing. Pam laughed so hard that tears were streaming down her face.

Lulu wasn't laughing. She was thinking, they should remember that horseback riding is serious business. *I'm never going to ride again. Never.*

Pony Pal Fight

Lulu blasted her whistle. Pam stopped, stood still, and tried to stop laughing. Anna climbed out of the sack and pulled up Acorn's head.

"What's wrong?" Pam asked.

"Why'd you blow the whistle?" asked Anna.

"You shouldn't fool around when you're working with ponies!" shouted Lulu. "Somebody could get hurt."

Pam went up to Anna and whispered in

her ear. Anna nodded and the two girls and their ponies walked over to Lulu.

"We need to have a Pony Pal Meeting right now," said Pam.

"About what?" asked Lulu.

"About *you*," said Anna. "You're not acting like yourself, Lulu. You're afraid of every little thing that has to do with riding."

Pam put her hand on Lulu's arm. "Lulu, you have to ride again," she said. "If you don't want to ride Paint, ride Splash. She's a nice calm pony. You won't be afraid on Splash."

Lulu shrugged Pam's hand off her arm. "I'm not afraid," she said. "I just don't want to ride today. Okay?"

"That's how I felt when I took a big fall last year," said Anna. "But Pam's mother made me get back on. And I'm glad she did."

"I'm *not* riding today," said Lulu. "I'll ride when Snow White is better. I'm taking her home now."

"I'll go with you," said Anna.

"Me, too," said Pam.

"I can do it myself," said Lulu, as she started to walk away.

"You're not acting like a Pony Pal," Anna called after her.

Lulu turned around and glared at Anna and Pam. "Just leave me alone," she shouted.

Anna glared back at Lulu. "We just wanted to help," she said angrily.

"Wait a minute!" ordered Pam.

"No!" shouted Lulu. She turned and left Pam and Anna standing in the field.

A minute later, Lulu came out of the barn with Snow White. She didn't even look over at the big field. Lulu didn't want to talk to Pam and Anna anymore. She wanted to take Snow White home.

Wet leaves covered Pony Pal Trail and Lulu held Snow White's lead rope shorter than usual. "Be careful, Snow White," she said. "Don't slip on the leaves." Snow White jerked her head. She was used to a

longer lead, but Lulu still held the rope short. "It's safer this way," she told her pony.

A squirrel ran across the trail in front of Lulu. It startled Snow White and she whinnied. Snow White pulled on the lead and snorted. "It's okay," Lulu told Snow White. "It was just a squirrel. It scared me, too.

"Pam and Lulu don't understand me anymore," Lulu told Snow White. "They don't know how awful it is to hurt your own pony."

As they went along the trail, Lulu noticed that Snow White was nervous and shied at the least little thing. This isn't such a great riding trail, thought Lulu. There are a lot of things a pony could slip or trip on. And the woods are filled with animals and birds that can spook a pony.

Lulu was glad when Pony Pal Trail came to an end and she could put Snow White in the paddock. "Now you're safe," she told Snow White.

Lulu stuffed fresh hay in Snow White's hay net and poured water into her bucket. She looked around to see what Snow White was doing. At the far end of the paddock, Lulu saw her pony grazing. She usually hangs around me when she's in the paddock, thought Lulu. She must really be upset about the accident.

Lulu went up to her pony. "The accident was my fault yesterday," she told Snow White. "I'm sorry it happened. I promise I'll never hurt you again."

Lulu left Snow White and went into the house. Her grandmother was in the kitchen making lunch. "Ah, Lulu's home," she said. She wrapped Lulu in a big hug. "How are you feeling?"

"Okay," said Lulu.

"I was watching you from the window," said Grandmother. "Snow White seems almost as good as new."

"She'll be okay," said Lulu. "We were lucky."

"You might not be so lucky the next time," said Grandmother.

"There won't be a next time," said Lulu. "I'm never going to ride again."

"Never!?" exclaimed her grandmother.

"Never," said Lulu. "I don't like riding anymore."

"Well, I certainly approve of that decision," said Grandmother. "But won't you miss riding with your friends? Won't you miss Snow White?"

"I'll still take care of Snow White," said Lulu. "But no one is going to ride her. Riding is dangerous for ponies."

"I see," said Grandmother slowly. "Do Anna and Pam know that you've given up riding?"

"Not yet," said Lulu. She didn't want to tell her grandmother about the Pony Pal fight.

After lunch, Lulu went up to her room. She lay down on her bed and closed her eyes. Anna's right, she thought. I'm not acting like a Pony Pal anymore. I don't even want to be one. Pam and Anna don't understand. *They* didn't have a serious accident. *They* didn't almost kill their pony. Snow White was her only Pony Pal. Would her pony ever forgive her?

Quitting

The next morning Lulu went out to the paddock to take care of Snow White. She was feeding her when Anna appeared carrying a big box.

"I'm sorry I yelled at you yesterday," said Anna. "Are you still angry at Pam and me?"

"I'm not angry," said Lulu. She didn't want to talk about not being a Pony Pal. At least not yet. She pointed to the box. "What's in there?" she asked.

"Art supplies," said Anna excitedly. "For making our costumes for the parade. Pam and I decided what we want to be. And we think the unicorn idea is perfect for Snow White. I've got the best idea for her horn."

"Hi!" a voice called. Lulu looked up. She saw Pam and Lightning coming off Pony Pal Trail. Anna ran over to open the gate for them. Then, after Pam had dismounted, she helped Pam take off Lightning's tack.

"The costume parade is going to be so much fun," said Anna. "It's going to take a lot of hard work, but I'm sure we'll be ready in time. Come on. I'll show Lulu the drawings and we can get started."

The Pony Pals sat at the picnic table near the paddock. Anna opened her art box, spread out some of the supplies, and pulled out a drawing. "Here's what Pam's going to be," she said. She handed the drawing to Lulu.

WE NEED:
FOR LIGHTNING
1. red felt blanket with black felt ladder
2. short water hose
3. red and black leg wraps

FOR PAM
1. yellow raincoat
2. Fireman's hat

"Isn't that great, Lulu!" exclaimed Anna.

"It's a terrific idea," said Lulu. "What are you going to be?"

Anna took another drawing out of the box and handed it to Lulu.

WE NEED:
FOR ACORN
1. wolf ears
2. rubber bands for the top and bottom of her tail

FOR ANNA
1. a red cape with hood
2. a straw hat
3. a checked cloth for the basket

"Ms. Wiggins is going to lend Anna her red cape for Little Red Riding Hood," said Pam.

"And I've got the cardboard and paint we

need to make the wolf ears," said Anna. "Ms. Wiggins said she'd come to the gymkhana to watch us, too."

Ms. Wiggins was a good friend of the Pony Pals. She had great trails on her property. The Pony Pals could ride there anytime they wanted.

Maybe I'll watch the games with Ms. Wiggins, thought Lulu. She looked at Anna's drawing again. "*Little Red Riding Hood* is a great idea," Lulu said.

Snow White whinnied. The three girls looked over at her. The pony walked a few feet and lowered her head to graze.

"She's fine," said Pam, looking at Lulu.

"I'm going to check on her anyway," said Lulu. She ran into the paddock. "Snow White," she called. "Are you okay?"

Snow White looked up. When she saw Lulu coming she turned and walked away from her.

Snow White hasn't forgiven me for the accident, thought Lulu. She doesn't trust me anymore. Lulu walked slowly back to the picnic table.

Anna held up a twisted wax candle. "Here's what I thought of for Snow White's horn," said Anna. The candle looked exactly like a unicorn's twisted horn.

"Isn't it perfect, Lulu?" asked Pam.

Lulu sat down at the picnic table with Anna and Pam. "Snow White isn't going to be a unicorn," she said.

"What's she going to be?" asked Anna.

Lulu took the candle from Anna and put it back in the box. "Snow White isn't going to be anything," answered Lulu. "We're not going to be in the costume parade. We're not going to be in the gymkhana."

"My dad said Snow White could," said Pam. "She can even practice this weekend."

"But if you want her to rest some more," said Anna, "you could still enter the games with Paint or Splash."

Lulu stood up. "I'm not riding Paint or

Splash either," said Lulu. "I'm not riding any ponies. Or horses. I quit riding."

"What!?" exclaimed Anna. She jumped up.

"*Not ride?*" said Pam. She stood up, too. "You can't quit riding, Lulu."

"Don't try to change my mind," said Lulu. "It won't work."

"You're just scared to ride because you fell," said Anna. "I was scared, too, after I fell off Acorn."

"Lulu, you fell off Snow White when we were practicing jumps," said Pam. "And you got back on. Why is this time different?"

"This time it was my fault!" shouted Lulu. "I almost killed Snow White and she knows it. She doesn't trust me anymore. She doesn't like me anymore."

"Lulu, that's not true," said Pam.

"It is," said Lulu. "It's all true. And the biggest true thing is that I'm not a Pony Pal anymore!"

Lulu turned and ran from her friends. She climbed over the fence and headed into the woods.

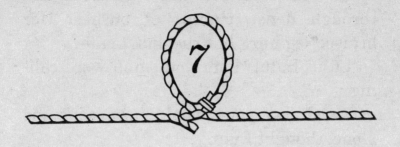

Breaking the Rules

Lulu wanted to be alone. She didn't want anyone to find her. So she went into the thickest, darkest part of the forest.

"Lulu stop!" Anna yelled.

"Come back," Pam shouted.

Lulu didn't stop and she didn't go back. She was running away. Running away from Pam and Anna who didn't understand her. Running away from the accident that was her fault. Running away from Snow White who didn't trust her anymore.

Lulu ran between tall pine trees and through dense clumps of bushes. Her bruised leg hurt, but she didn't care.

"Lulu! Lulu!" Pam and Anna were calling.

I wish everyone would just leave me alone, thought Lulu.

Lulu's chest hurt from running. She stopped and listened. She couldn't hear Pam's and Anna's voices anymore. She leaned against a tree and looked up. She could barely see the sky through the treetops. She looked around. She was surrounded by hundreds of trees. There wasn't a trail in sight.

I don't know where I am, she thought. And I don't care. I don't care about Pony Pals. I don't care about anything.

Lulu heard the faint blasts of a whistle. Anna and Pam were signaling her. They were still looking for her. I won't let them find me, thought Lulu. I have to hide. She plunged deeper into the woods.

Lulu remembered the *Safety in the Woods* rules her father taught her.

1. Hike with a buddy.
2. Tell someone where you are going and when you will be back.
3. Bring water, snacks, a whistle, and a flashlight.
4. Hike only on familiar or marked trails.
5. Bring an extra layer of clothing and raingear.

Lulu knew that she was breaking all the *Safety in the Woods* rules. But she didn't care. She kept walking. And walking. And walking. She stopped and listened again. She didn't hear the blasts of Pam's and Anna's whistles anymore.

Lulu sat down on the pine-covered floor of the forest. It was so dark in the woods that she thought it was night. I don't care if I stay out all night, she thought. I'm not going back. Lulu looked at the hands of her glow-in-the-dark watch. It was only eleven-thirty in the morning! She looked up. The little bits of sky that showed between the treetops were dark and heavy with clouds.

Suddenly, a streak of lightning lit up the woods. It was followed by a crack of thunder. Lulu felt raindrops on her face.

The rain fell harder. Lulu's clothes and hair were getting wet. And it was cold. She shivered. Soon her shirt and hair were soaked with rainwater and her teeth chattered from the cold. I don't care if I freeze to death, she thought. I'm not going back.

Another flash of lightning lit up the woods. The sound of thunder boomed around Lulu. The lightning seemed closer.

Lulu heard another sound in the distance — the blasts of whistles. Pam and Anna were still looking for her. I don't want them to find me, thought Lulu. I have to go deeper into the woods. She ran away from the sounds of the whistles.

Lulu knew that Pam and Anna would keep looking for her. They wouldn't turn back. They were Pony Pals. And the Pony Pals *never gave up.*

She listened more carefully. Three blasts. It was the Pony Pal SOS signal. Were Pam and Anna in trouble?

Lulu tried to see where she was in the dark woods. Nothing looked familiar. She was lost. Anna and Pam must be lost, too, thought Lulu. They were probably wet and cold. But they were still looking for her instead of trying to find their way home. If anything happened to Anna and Pam it would be her fault.

Lulu was the Pony Pal who knew the most about being out in the woods. She had to find them. She had to help them get home.

Wind howled through the trees. I have to stay calm, Lulu thought. She quickly checked her jeans pockets. She had her whistle, too. Taking a deep breath, Lulu blew a loud blast. Another blast answered it! She listened for the direction of the sound and walked toward the sound.

Lulu heard her friends calling her name. She called back. "Pam. Anna."

"We're here," Pam shouted back.

Lulu looked past the dark tree trunks in front of her. She saw the shape of two small figures between the tall pines. It was Pam and Anna!

Lulu ran toward them. And they ran toward her. The three friends hugged in the middle of the dark forest.

"Are you okay?" asked Pam.

"We were so afraid you were lost," said Anna.

"I *am* lost," said Lulu.

"So are we," said Pam.

The three friends looked at one another through the pelting rain. They all knew how dangerous it was to be lost in the woods, especially in a storm.

Lightning lit up the woods again. Lulu knew it was her fault that they were all lost. She had to save her friends. She had to find a way out of the woods.

Badd Brook

"Don't worry," Lulu told Pam and Anna. "I'll get us home." Lulu knew she had to forget about all her other problems. She had to concentrate.

The three girls huddled together in the rain. "First, we have to figure out where we are," said Lulu. "Have either of you noticed anything familiar? Like a rock ledge? Or a brook or pond?"

"I think I saw Lake Appamapog during the last flash of lightning," said Anna.

"Where?" asked Lulu excitedly.

Anna pointed to her left.

"Let's go in that direction," said Lulu.

"We don't live anywhere near the lake, Lulu," said Pam.

"But Badd Brook runs into the lake," said Lulu. "If we find the lake, we can find Badd Brook. Badd Brook also crosses Pony Pal Trail. So if we follow Badd Brook, it will lead us to Pony Pal Trail."

"Good thinking," said Pam. "Let's go."

Anna led the way. During the next flash of lightning Lulu saw the lake, too. Minutes later the three girls were standing on the shore of Lake Appamapog.

"Look for places on the lake that you know," said Lulu. "That will help us figure out where to find the end of Badd Brook."

Pam pointed to her left. "There's the town beach," she said. "But it's far away."

Anna pointed across the lake. "And I think I see Ms. Wiggins' house," she said.

Lulu pointed to her right. "Then the brook is in that direction. It shouldn't be too far."

The girls walked through the woods along the edge of the lake. They came to the place where the brook flowed into it.

"Now all we have to do is follow the brook to Pony Pal Trail," said Lulu. "Let's go."

The woods were dense along the brook. It took the three girls over an hour to reach Pony Pal Trail. They were wet, tired, and cold. But they were very happy to be on the familiar trail.

"I wonder if anyone is looking for us," said Anna.

"I bet our ponies are," said Pam. "We've been away a long time."

"Lulu, did you really mean it when you said you're not going to ride?" asked Anna.

Lulu nodded. "I'm not a good rider," she said. "And Snow White doesn't trust me anymore."

"But Lulu . . ." Pam started to say.

Lulu interrupted her. "I don't want to talk about it," she said. "I only stopped running away because *you* were lost. I had to help you. I didn't want to hurt anyone else.

I've already hurt Snow White. But I'm not a Pony Pal anymore. The end."

"You don't have to ride to be a Pony Pal," said Anna.

"I know," said Lulu. "But I don't *want* to be a Pony Pal."

Pam and Anna exchanged a glance. They silently agreed not to argue with Lulu.

When the girls finally got back to the Harleys, Lightning and Acorn came over to greet Pam and Anna. But Snow White stayed where she was at the far end of the paddock. Lulu walked toward her pony. She wanted to be sure Snow White was okay after the storm. "Come here, Snow White," she said softly. "Come see me."

Snow White ignored Lulu. Lulu moved a little closer. "I won't hurt you," she said. Snow White turned and walked away from Lulu.

Lulu ran to her house. This time Anna and Pam didn't try to follow her. Pam and Anna saw for themselves that Snow White doesn't like me anymore, thought Lulu.

They finally understand why I can't be a Pony Pal anymore.

Lulu took a hot bath and put on dry clothes. She decided that she would read a book to take her mind off her problems. She looked across the titles of the books on her bookshelf. They were all about ponies and horses. She didn't want to read about ponies and horses anymore.

"Hi," said a voice. Lulu looked up. Anna and Pam were standing at her bedroom door.

"Hi," said Lulu.

"We're going to the diner for lunch," said Anna. "We want you to come."

Lulu remembered how her friends had followed her into the woods. She remembered how they got lost in a storm because of her.

"I'll go to lunch," said Lulu. "But I'm finished being a Pony Pal."

"You already told us that," said Anna. "About a thousand times."

*   *   *

Anna's mother owned the Off-Main Diner, so the Pony Pals could eat there for free. But they had to be their own waiters. They ordered grilled cheese sandwiches with french fries, apple juice, and brownies.

They took their food to their favorite booth. While they ate they talked about being lost and finding their way out of the woods.

"It's a good thing you saw the lake," Lulu told Anna. "I had *no* idea where we were."

"But Lulu had the idea to follow the brook," said Pam. "That was brilliant."

"Well, it was my fault in the first place," said Lulu. "I'm sorry."

"That's okay," said Anna. "It ended up being an adventure."

"We know you aren't a Pony Pal anymore, Lulu," said Pam. "But Anna and I have our biggest Pony Pal Problem ever. So we're having a Pony Pal Meeting to share our ideas."

"I suppose the problem is me," said Lulu.

"You and Snow White," said Pam.

Lulu stood up. "I told you I don't want to talk about Pony Pals," she said. "I'm going."

Anna grabbed the end of Lulu's sweater so she couldn't go. "Sit down and listen," she said firmly. She added, "Please." Lulu saw tears in Anna's eyes.

I'll listen, thought Lulu. But this is a problem even the Pony Pals can't solve.

Two Ideas

Lulu sat back down in the booth. "Snow White doesn't trust me anymore," she told Pam and Anna. "You saw how she ran away from me."

"I think I know why Snow White did that," said Pam. "That's what my idea is about." Pam took out a piece of paper and read:

Snow White is acting weird because you are not being her leader.

"You used to be her leader," said Pam. "But since the accident you act afraid around her. You don't tell her what to do."

"When Acorn wouldn't jump for me, I had to show him that I was the boss," said Anna.

"Snow White has to know that you are in charge, Lulu," said Anna. "She wants you to take care of her."

"But I *didn't* take care of Snow White," said Lulu. "Remember the accident."

"Since the accident you've been acting like someone who doesn't know how to handle a pony," said Pam. "That's not good for Snow White."

"Act the way you used to act with her," said Anna.

Lulu thought about Pam's idea for a minute. Finally she said, "I'll try your idea, Pam. But I still won't ride."

"Riding is what my idea is about," said Anna. She put a drawing on the table. Lulu and Pam looked at it.

"Snow White misses riding and being with *her* Pony Pals," said Anna.

"We don't want to leave Snow White behind when we go riding," said Pam.

"But I don't want to ride anymore," said Lulu.

"That's because you're afraid," said Pam. "The longer you wait to get back on a pony, the more afraid you are going to be."

Anna leaned forward. "Snow White doesn't understand why you're not riding her," she said.

"I don't think she wants me to ride her," said Lulu.

"You won't know unless you try," said Anna.

Lulu stood up. "Okay," she said, "I'll try both of your ideas."

Anna smiled at Lulu. "And if they work, will you be a Pony Pal again?" she asked.

"*If* they work," said Lulu. "That's a big *if*."

The girls cleared the table and walked back to the Harley paddock.

"Remember, treat Snow White the way you always did," Pam reminded Lulu.

Lulu approached her pony. "Hi, Snow White," Lulu said in a confident voice.

Snow White looked up at Lulu.

"Come here," said Lulu firmly. She

71

walked toward Snow White. I'm in charge, Lulu told herself. Snow White has to pay attention to me.

Lulu put her hand on Snow White's neck. "You're a good pony," she said in a strong voice.

Snow White nuzzled Lulu's shoulder. Lulu patted Snow White's head. "I'm putting on your halter now," said Lulu. "Stay still." Snow White stayed still while Lulu slipped on her halter and clipped on the lead rope. "Let's go," she said firmly.

Snow White walked behind Lulu. She nickered happily as if to say, "My leader is back!"

"Let's go for a trail ride, Lulu," Anna yelled.

Lulu felt her heart beat faster. I'm afraid, she thought. I'm afraid to ride my own pony.

"Maybe tomorrow," Lulu called back.

"We're taking our ponies on a trail ride

now," said Pam. "Snow White will wonder why she can't go, too."

Lulu looked at her beautiful, strong pony. Snow White loved to go on trail rides with her Pony Pals. I have to ride, Lulu thought. I have to do it for Snow White.

"Okay," said Lulu. "We'll ride with you."

"Great!" shouted Pam and Anna.

The three girls saddled up their ponies. Lulu still felt afraid of riding.

"You mount first, Lulu," said Pam. "You should ride around the field before we go on the trail."

"Okay," said Lulu.

Anna held Lightning's and Acorn's bridles. Pam went over to Lulu. "Even if you're afraid," she told Lulu, "act like you aren't."

"Do it for Snow White," said Anna.

Lulu pulled the reins over Snow White's head. Her hands were cold and sweaty. She stood next to her pony and faced the saddle. I can do it, Lulu said to herself. I can do it. I can. I can do it for Snow White. She put her left foot in the stirrup.

"I'll give you a leg up," said Pam.

"I can do it," said Lulu. She stood on the left stirrup and swung her right leg over the saddle. She was sitting on Snow White.

"Let's go," Lulu told her pony.

The first thing Lulu did was walk Snow White around the field. When Snow White acted lazy, Lulu made her walk faster. The second time around the field she moved Snow White into a trot. Lulu had never felt afraid on a pony before but now she had a nervous feeling in her stomach. She wondered if she would ever ride again without being afraid.

Ponies on Parade

Lulu rode Snow White a little longer each day that week. Each time she still felt that nervous feeling in her stomach.

Over the weekend the girls practiced gymkhana games at Pam's house. Anna and Pam laughed and had a good time practicing the pony games. Lulu tried to join them. She tried remembering how much she loved the games at the gymkhanas in England. But now she wasn't even having fun practicing her favorite game — the Sack Race. Lulu didn't want to practice any games where Snow White had to weave in and out of bending poles.

The night before the games the Pony Pals had a barn sleepover. They woke up very early and gave their ponies a special grooming. Lulu rubbed Snow White's coat to a shine. "Don't worry," Lulu whispered in Snow White's ear, "we'll be extra careful when we play the games. We won't get hurt."

At eight o'clock the Pony Pals rode to Mr. Olson's horse farm for the gymkhana. Grandmother Sanders brought their costumes for the parade in her car.

The big field at Mr. Olson's horse farm was all prepared for a gymkhana. Lulu saw four rows of bending poles lined up in the field. A big crowd was gathering to watch the games. "This is going to be so much fun," said Anna. Maybe for you, Lulu thought. But not for me.

Mr. Olson came over to the Pony Pals. "The first game is the Bending Race," he told them. "We're playing this game in relay teams of three players. I guess you three want to be a team."

"A relay race!" exclaimed Lulu. "Would we all have to do the Bending Race?"

"Of course," said Mr. Olson. "First, one rider goes. She's carrying a stick. At the finish line she hands the stick to the next rider, and the second rider goes. When the third rider on the team finishes, we see which team won the race. It's a team effort."

"I know what a relay race is," said Lulu. "But I don't like to do the Bending Race."

"We can't be in that race," Pam told Mr. Olson.

"That's too bad," he said. "A lot of the games today are relay races. I guess I should have put that on the poster." He turned to get the games started.

Lulu could see that Anna and Pam were disappointed. Lulu hadn't done the Bending Race since the accident and she didn't want to do that race. But the Pony Pals need me, she thought. They can't enter the race with just two riders.

Lulu swallowed hard and took a deep breath. "Wait, Mr. Olson," she said. "Put the Pony Pals down as a relay team for the Bending Race."

"Are you sure, Lulu?" asked Pam.

"Yes," said Lulu. "I'm a Pony Pal. We should be in this race together."

Anna and Pam grinned at Lulu.

"Yeah," said Anna.

"Come on, Pony Pals," said Pam. "Let's win this race."

Lulu smiled at her friends. It felt great to be a Pony Pal again.

There were four teams of three riders for Bending Poles. Pam was the first rider for the Pony Pal team. She came across the finish line first. The Pony Pals were ahead.

Anna took the stick from Pam. She and Acorn rode in and out of the poles at a gallop.

"Go, Anna!" shouted Lulu. "Go, Acorn!" But the rider from the fourth team was faster than Anna and Acorn and came across the finish line first. The Pony Pals were in second place. It was up to Lulu.

Anna handed the stick to Lulu. "Go," shouted Anna.

"Go!" Lulu shouted to Snow White. She gave her pony the signal to gallop. But she didn't need to tell Snow White what to do. Snow White *wanted* to gallop fast. She wanted to win the race. Lulu and Snow White bent around the poles, turned, and galloped back. They flew across the finish line before the other rider.

Lulu halted Snow White. She leaned over and patted her pony's sweaty neck. "Good work, Snow White," she said.

"We won!" shouted Anna. "You did it, Lulu!"

"Snow White did it!" exclaimed Lulu. She burst out laughing.

"What's so funny?" asked Pam.

"Nothing," said Lulu. "I'm just happy that I wasn't afraid. I did the Bending Race and I wasn't afraid. It was fun!"

The Pony Pals pulled their ponies up to

one another. They lifted their hands and hit high fives. "All-*right*!" they shouted.

"The next game is Egg and Spoon," announced Mr. Olson. "Relay race with teams of three."

"Let's go," said Lulu. "Maybe we can win this one, too."

Pam dropped the egg during her turn. She had to dismount and put it back on the spoon. The Pony Pals came in third in the Egg and Spoon game. But they didn't care. They were having fun.

The Pony Pals came in last for the Sack Race. Acorn was sure that Anna's sack was filled with grain just for him. Everyone watching the gymkhana was laughing. Lulu laughed so hard her sides hurt.

After the Sack Race, the Pony Pals had fifteen minutes to get ready for the costume parade. They changed into their costumes in the Crandals' horse trailer. Lulu put on white tights and the white gown her grandmother had found for her in the attic. She wrapped silver ribbons around her black riding boots. Lulu felt like a princess and went outside to make Snow White into a unicorn.

Lulu changed Snow White's blanket to a white one that was trimmed with lace. She scattered silver sparkles on Snow White's coat, tied a big lace ribbon around her tail, and hooked the twisted white candle to the bridle. Snow White was used to the costume because Lulu had put it on her for practice. Lulu put a lace cover on her helmet and put the helmet on. The princess and the unicorn were ready.

Lulu looked over at Anna. "You make a *perfect* Little Red Riding Hood and the Wolf," Lulu told Anna and Acorn.

"And look at Pam and Lightning," said Anna.

Lulu had to smile when she saw the firefighter on her truck.

As the Pony Pals were lining up, Acorn turned around and tried to get an apple from Little Red Riding Hood's basket.

Anna made Acorn behave. Lulu giggled. She was having a great time.

Mr. Olson came over to Lulu. "I think the unicorn should start off the parade," he told her.

Lulu was happy. She knew that Snow White would love leading a parade.

Lulu pulled Snow White up to the front of the line. Mr. Olson gave Lulu the signal and the parade began. As Lulu trotted Snow White around the field she heard the viewers go "oo-hh" and "ah-hh." Grandmother Sanders was standing with Ms. Wiggins. They both smiled and waved to her. Lulu heard somebody say, "Isn't that white pony a beauty. She's a perfect pony."

Snow White is a perfect pony, thought Lulu proudly.

Out of the corner of her eye, Lulu could see Anna-the-firefighter and Pam-Little-Red-Riding-Hood on their ponies. They looked perfect, too.

"We're Pony Pals," Lulu told Snow White. "Pony Pals forever."

Dear Reader:

I am having a lot of fun researching and writing books about the Pony Pals. I've met many interesting kids and adults who love ponies. And I've visited some wonderful ponies at homes, farms, and riding schools.

Before writing Pony Pals I wrote fourteen novels for children and young adults. Four of these were honored by Children's Choice Awards.

I live in Sharon, Connecticut, with my husband, Lee, and our dog, Willie. Our daughter is all grown up and has her own apartment in New York City.

Besides writing novels I like to draw, paint, garden, and swim. I didn't have a pony when I was growing up, but I have always loved them and dreamt about riding. Now I take riding lessons on a horse named Saz.

I like reading and writing about ponies as much as I do riding. Which proves to me that you don't have to ride a pony to love them. And you certainly don't need a pony to be a Pony Pal.

Happy Reading,

Jeanne Betancourt